D0717976

The Boy
Who
Sprouted
Antlers

The Boy Who Sprouted Antlers

by John Yeoman
illustrated by Quentin Blake

Thames & Hudson

OFFALY LIBRARY	
~~30013005356002~~	
Bertrams	12/10/2018
JF	
DG	02356011

PUBLISHER'S NOTE

*T*he Boy Who Sprouted Antlers is a sparkling, magical tale for children created from the fertile, ever-inventive minds of John Yeoman and Quentin Blake, who have now been collaborating on their many wonderful books for well over 50 years. It's a thrill to be able to republish this gem of a book – with all its surreal flights of fancy in word and drawing – just as it was originally intended and to let a new generation of children (and adults!) discover this fresh and inspiring tale of the triumph of imagination.

Roger Thorp

FOREWORD

In 1960 John Yeoman and I published *A Drink of Water;* our first book together and also the first book I had illustrated. We found we enjoyed the experience, and wanted to try it again. This time, John's subject came not from his reading but from his imagination: a fantasy with detail observed from the reality of school life. It is also the only book that I have illustrated twice, since within ten years boys started wearing long trousers and a new edition was called for. The first version has now become something of a period piece, but we hope that, even in short trousers, it will be no less enjoyable.

Quentin Blake

It was a fine afternoon at the beginning of the summer term and the sunlight streaming through the large windows of the classroom distracted Billy Dexter from the basket that he was supposed to be making. Miss Beddows, the form mistress of Class 2 of the Juniors of Burrow Road Primary (Mixed) School, was keeping a careful eye on the children who were out at the front selecting lengths of cane and soaking them in the large basin of water. From time to time she looked up to see how the children were getting on with their baskets. At last she stood up and walked slowly between the rows of desks, picking up an unfinished basket here and there, turning it over in her hands and replacing it on the desk with a satisfied 'Well done, Gloria' or 'That's coming along nicely, Francis.'

But when she came to the desk where Billy Dexter and Jacek Volkovinsky sat she stopped suddenly and gasped. All eyes in the form-room turned to the misshapen basket which she was now holding in her hand.

'*What* do you call this, Billy Dexter?' she asked in a quavering voice, as if unable to believe her eyes. 'What *do* you call this?'

It was certainly a poor attempt at a basket. Billy had had some difficulty with the sides, which refused to remain upright, and had gone under several times when he should have gone over, and over when he should have gone under. He would have blamed it on the fine weather, but it was no use telling Miss Beddows that.

'I have never seen such messy, careless, untidy work,' continued Miss Beddows, hastily unpicking with her long, tapering fingers everything that Billy had done in the last three hand-work lessons, as if she couldn't bear the sight of it.

'A boy who can't do better than this,' she said, waving the spidery remains of the basket in the air, 'doesn't deserve to be a milk monitor. Patrick Ives, you will be milk monitor in Billy Dexter's place for the rest of the week. And *you*, Billy Dexter, will stay behind after school.'

The half-finished baskets and the basketry materials were collected up quietly and taken off to the craft store-room and then the bell rang. The class sat perfectly still for a minute (because Miss Beddows wasn't going to let them out until everyone was quiet and ready, and *someone* was spoiling it) before filing out onto the open verandah, where everyone burst into shouts and raced off home.

Everyone, that is, except Melanie Pearce and Paul Hillary, who usually went home with Billy and stood outside waiting

11

for him now. Billy sat patiently, looking out of the window at his friends, until Miss Beddows, who had been writing something in order to keep him waiting, looked up and attracted his attention with a dry cough.

'Well, Billy Dexter, what have you to say for yourself? Why are you slacking like this? There is no doubt about it, your work is getting worse and worse. And why? You are just not concentrating anymore. The work isn't too difficult for you; you can do it if you try.'

Billy hadn't spoken at first because she seemed happy to answer her own questions, but now he felt he must say something.

'I understand the sums better now,' he said. 'I think I can do them. But I'll never be able to make a basket. The sides go all wonky when I do it.'

'I've never heard such nonsense,' replied Miss Beddows, who clearly wasn't angry anymore. 'Of course you can make a basket if you put your mind to it. You're a clever boy, really. You can make a basket as well as the next boy.' Miss Beddows had forgotten that Jacek Volkovinsky was the next boy, but Billy understood that she intended it kindly.

'Now remember, I expect to see a great improvement in your work. I want to hear no more of this nonsense about not being able to do it. As long as you set your mind on it and try hard enough there's nothing you can't do.' And with that she let him go.

Billy found this all very encouraging. 'Did she spout the usual bilge?' asked the impatient Melanie, who often used very unlady-like language.

'No,' said Billy, 'she told me there's nothing I can't do if I try hard.'

'That's the usual bilge,' replied Melanie, as they went out of the school gates and turned into Watermore Avenue.

'It certainly seems rather a stupid thing to say,' agreed Paul. 'After all, there must be heaps of things you can't do, no matter how hard you try.'

'What, for instance?' demanded Billy, who liked the idea of his being able to do anything.

'Like climb Everest or break the air speed record,' replied Paul, as they went into Freeman's to buy their iced lollies. Paul could have added many other items to the list of things that Billy couldn't do, but he was satisfied that this was enough to keep him quiet.

They bought their iced lollies, lemon flavour, and came out into the sunshine again.

'But people have climbed Everest and people do break the air speed record,' argued Billy, 'and that proves that it can be done. It just happens that I don't want to do it. They did want to and that's why they could do it.'

Melanie took a long, noisy suck at her lolly, extracting a lot of lemon flavour and leaving a colourless and tasteless frosty patch.

'What about growing horns, then?' she challenged. It was the sort of stupid remark that you expected of her. 'It's no use saying that other people have grown horns because they haven't. And it's no use saying you could if you wanted to, because we know you couldn't.'

Billy was taken aback. The idea was so ridiculous.

'She's right,' said Paul, a little annoyed that Billy had pushed his argument aside.

'I still say that I could,' began Billy.

'... if you wanted to,' continued Paul.

'And, of course, you don't want to,' added Melanie. It was clear from her smile that she thought she had won.

'I will, then!' shouted Billy, immediately aware that it was a silly thing to say.

Melanie and Paul were delighted. 'Go on, then,' they cried. 'Let's see you,' said Melanie.

'Well, you don't expect me to grow them *here*, do you?' said Billy, wishing he'd never started the argument. 'You've got to give me time. It may take days, or even weeks. You can't expect a person to grow horns on the spot, just like that. You have to set your mind on it. It takes a lot of effort.'

Paul and Melanie laughed in a good-humoured way. They were rather pleased that Billy found himself in this awkward position and they wanted to make the most of it. 'Oh, there's no hurry,' said Paul.

'But you will let us know how your horns are coming along, won't you,' said Melanie with mock solemnity, as she tried to suppress a smile.

'You don't know anything about it!' shouted Billy. 'You're laughing now, but just you wait and see.'

Paul and Melanie didn't want to talk about it any longer. They said 'Good-bye' and disappeared down Repton Road, still highly amused.

*   *   *   *

Billy walked on by himself, thinking things over. He was going to look pretty silly in a few weeks' time if he still hadn't managed to grow any horns. He knew that if he failed Melanie wouldn't let him hear the last of it. And although he had been quite confident immediately after his talk with Miss Beddows, he was less certain of himself now.

'There's nothing for it, I shall just have to grow horns,' he said aloud, much to the surprise of an elderly lady who happened to be passing.

'If the next bus to pass me is a 51, that means that I will certainly be able to do it. If it's a 51A, then *perhaps* I can do it. If it's anything else I'll give up,' he went on.

The number of the approaching bus was getting clearer. It was a 51. But before the bus could reach him another bus, also a 51, passed Billy from behind.

'Two 51s! That means I can't fail,' he thought triumphantly. 'But to make quite sure, I won't step on any cracks from now on until I get home.'

He turned right into Spur Road, stepping deliberately in the middle of each paving stone. He reached his front door without having stepped on any of the lines.

*   *   *   *

There was an uncomfortable moment after tea when, chanting 'Yes, no, perhaps' over the pips of an orange that he had just eaten, he ended up on the word 'perhaps'. Luckily, he found another pip which he must have dropped on the floor.

He didn't go out to play that evening. In fact, he was very eager to get to bed, asking his mother several times if it was nearly bedtime.

'I don't think the boy's feeling very well,' said Mrs Dexter to her husband when Billy had gone upstairs.

'Why, what's up?' asked Mr Dexter, still reading his evening paper.

Mrs Dexter turned the sound of the television down to make conversation easier.

'Well, he seems to have been daydreaming ever since he came in from school, and he didn't mind going off to bed,' she said, in an anxious voice.

'Probably got something on his mind. I'd give him an aspirin. He'll be as right as rain in the morning if you give him an aspirin.' And with that Mr Dexter turned up the sound of the television again and went back to his evening paper.

Mrs Dexter fetched a glass of water and an aspirin, and opened the door of Billy's small bedroom just in time to hear him mumbling: '... nine hundred and ninety-seven, nine hundred and ninety-eight, nine hundred and ninety-nine, one thousand.'

'You shouldn't be singing if you've got a headache,' she said, handing him the glass of water.

'I haven't got a headache,' said Billy, sitting up in bed.

'It'll only make it worse if you sing. Here, I've brought you an aspirin. Don't scratch your head, love. Why are all

your model aeroplanes upside down?' said Mrs Dexter. And she moved over to where Billy had arranged his models on the floor and turned one of them up the right way.

'No special reason,' said Billy, untruthfully, and snuggled down into the sheets again.

As soon as Mrs Dexter had said 'Good night' and he had heard her go downstairs, Billy leapt out of bed and turned the aeroplane upside down again. He didn't want to spoil things at this stage, especially as the signs had been so good that evening. He had found the letters that spelled his name from the front page of his father's paper and the number of matches in the matchbox on the dining-room mantelpiece had come to 'Yes'. Turning all this over in his mind he crept back into bed and soon fell asleep.

*   *   *   *

Next morning Mrs Dexter woke him at the usual time.

'Get up, Billy,' she called as she opened his curtains to let the light in. 'It's a fine morning and ... Do leave your head alone. Does it ache?' she asked anxiously. She took Billy's hand from his head and put her own in its place. The expression on her face told Billy what he wanted to know.

'You've got a bump, Billy. *Two* bumps. Have you got a headache, love? Let's feel your forehead. Did you hit your head at school yesterday? You haven't been fighting now, have you, Billy?'

19

'I feel all right,' replied Billy. 'I remember, I was hit over the head with *Janet and John Book Three* yesterday, but it didn't hurt.'

'It could be that,' said Mrs Dexter doubtfully.

'But I don't think it is,' said Billy. 'It's a very soft book. I feel quite well,' he added, to set his mother's mind at rest.

Mr Dexter felt the bumps and decided that Billy should be sent to school with a note asking the teacher to let him come home early if he felt ill.

Billy couldn't get to Repton Road quickly enough. He broke the news to Melanie and Paul, who were there waiting for him and let them inspect his head. It was clear that they were convinced that Billy had started growing horns. Paul apologised generously and added that he thought that Billy had done extremely well in such a short time.

'Shall we keep it to ourselves?' asked Melanie, who was overjoyed with the thought that it was her idea in the first place.

'Let's keep it a secret for the moment,' suggested Billy who, though delighted at his success, was a little worried at the way the grown-ups would receive the news.

His plan pleased the others, however, as it gave them the double pleasure of sharing a special secret for a few days and of being the first to tell the news when the time came.

Billy put on his school cap again and they went on their way.

In class that morning Billy sat engrossed in his thoughts. He didn't hear a word that Miss Beddows said, and he was rebuked several times for fidgeting when his hand went to his head to discover the progress of his horns. He was flushed with success. How could anyone think that being a milk monitor mattered?

At the mid-morning break Billy drank his milk quickly and went out on to the school field with Melanie, Paul, Jacek and Tommy Mullins. The three found the greatest difficulty in talking about other things, but the horns couldn't be mentioned in front of Jacek and Tommy. They had to be content with exchanging knowing glances.

When the whistle went they lined up in the playground and Melanie contrived to be Billy's partner at the very end of the row. The whistle went again and Miss Beddows led them, in silence, along the verandah to their classroom. Melanie made Billy drop back a little and whispered excitedly: 'You won't be able to keep them a secret much longer. They're beginning to show!' And it was perfectly true.

*　　*　　*　　*

In class Miss Beddows asked Billy if his bumps had gone down. He couldn't truthfully say that they had, and while he was thinking of an answer Miss Beddows put her hand on his head. She withdrew it immediately and her eyebrows arched high above her rimless spectacles.

'Are you sure you feel well, Billy?' she asked anxiously. 'The bumps are *very* large.'

At this Melanie nudged Paul and winked confidentially at Billy. Billy assured Miss Beddows that he was feeling quite well, but she nevertheless bundled him off to the headmaster, Mr Bartholemew, with a note.

Mr Bartholemew also raised his eyebrows and asked the same question, and then decided that Billy should go home with another note telling his mother that it would be just as well to call a doctor if the bumps didn't disappear soon.

Mrs Dexter had just got in from shopping when Billy arrived home with his note. She looked worried, sent him up to bed (much against his will this time) and rushed round to Mrs Peacock, who was on the phone, to call the doctor. The doctor said he would come in the evening.

Billy passed the rest of the morning and the afternoon in a state of boredom. He was too excited about the horns to be able to read or draw, and now he was being deprived of the opportunity to enjoy the success of his efforts. He wondered if he should explain everything to his mother, but on second thoughts decided that she would be more willing to believe the doctor when he told her that there was nothing to worry about.

At last evening came, and Dr Preston arrived.

'What seems to be the trouble?' he called cheerily, as he burst into Billy's room. But there could be no question now of what the 'trouble' was. There were two small, but unmistakable horns on Billy's head, for all to see. Mrs Dexter, of course, continued to refer to them as bumps, but Billy could tell from the look of bewilderment on Dr Preston's face that *he* knew the truth.

'Yes. Bumps. Yes, rather large bumps.' He was clearly put out. He fingered them gingerly, felt Billy's pulse, inspected the horns again, took Billy's temperature, looked at his tongue, listened to his heart, tapped the horns with his forefinger and turned to Mrs Dexter with acute embarrassment.

'I am, er, happy to tell you that there is nothing, er, wrong – actually wrong – with the boy. His temperature, pulse and ...' he began hesitantly.

'But what about those bumps, doctor?' said Mrs Dexter.

'Yes, I was coming to that. Now that I am quite satisfied that the boy is well in himself, as we might say, I feel that I would like a second opinion on the precise nature of the, er, bumps and therefore ...'

'You mean you're sending Billy to a specialist?' asked Mrs Dexter, somewhat reassured by the news.

'To a vet, actually,' said Dr Preston apologetically, in a half-whisper, as he ushered Mrs Dexter out of the bedroom.

But Billy had heard and his excitement knew no bounds.

*   *   *   *

The next morning Mrs Dexter announced solemnly to Billy, whose horns were now about two inches long, that they were going to see a specialist. She said 'specialist' because she didn't want to hurt Billy's feelings, and he didn't contradict her because he didn't want to hurt hers.

They got to the vet's quite early, but there were already three other people in the waiting room when they arrived. There was a woman with a goldfish in a polythene bag filled with water, a man with a tabby cat with one of its front legs in plaster, and another woman with a Pekingese on her lap. They sat in a row, waiting their turn.

The bell above the door tinkled as Billy and his mother entered the waiting room and a young lady receptionist in a white coat appeared.

'And what have you come about?' she asked with a pleasant smile. She looked round for the animal and, seeing none, wondered if Billy had brought a mouse in his pocket.

Mrs Dexter looked embarrassed and silently mouthed something to the receptionist.

24

'I'm very sorry, madam, I didn't quite catch ...'

Mrs Dexter plucked up courage and lifted Billy's school cap from his head. Billy glowed with satisfaction as he watched the receptionist's eyebrows.

Billy and his mother took their place in the queue, Billy sitting next to the lady with the Peke.

'Wouldn't you like to put your cap on again?' asked Mrs Dexter, offering it to him.

'No, thank you,' said Billy blandly, 'it's not polite to wear a cap indoors.'

Just then the Peke started behaving in a strange manner. It began yapping and snarling at Billy, despite its owner's attempts to calm it, and finally leapt from her lap to the floor and tried to seize Billy by the ankle. And then Billy did an extraordinary thing. Instead of kicking the noisy little animal away, he dropped down on all fours and butted the Peke with all his might. The dog yelped and fled into the corner of the room.

Fortunately, Mrs Dexter was rescued from her confusion by the reappearance of the receptionist, who announced that the vet had requested to see Billy next.

Mr Hanson, the vet, was the first grown-up who seemed pleased with Billy's good work.

'Perfect!' he cried, after examining Billy. 'There's absolutely nothing to worry about, madam. It should be a very fine pair, a very fine pair indeed. The boy is quite healthy: his coat is in good condition and his nose is cold. See to it that he gets plenty of green stuff in his diet and give him one of these tablets in his drinking water every day.'

He handed her a little box of tablets.

'By all means keep him at home for the rest of the day if you wish, but he must go to school tomorrow. I would like to see him in a week's time, and please ring me up if you notice any development before then.'

And with this he showed Mrs Dexter and Billy to the door. 'I've seen hundreds of these cases,' he told them, although he didn't mention that this was the first time the patient had been a human being.

The vet was overjoyed when, that very evening, he had a phone call from Mr Dexter to say that there *had* been a

development. The horns were starting to sprout in all directions.

*   *   *   *

Strange as it may seem, Mrs Dexter was beginning to feel more at ease now. She was relieved that no one thought there was any cause for anxiety but, of course, she was still rather bewildered. The important thing was that Billy wasn't in the least upset about his new antlers, and she could see that Mr Dexter was taking the whole thing very calmly. In fact, his first words on seeing Billy's fresh branches had been, 'I reckon we'd better pull his bed away from the wall and take off the headboard, just in case they grow any more during the night.'

Mrs Dexter did as the vet had advised and sent the excited Billy off to school the next day. But she told him to go straight to Mr Bartholemew and give him the note that she'd written.

Billy held his head high as he walked to school because he was so proud of his antlers and because his school cap, which, regulations stated, had to be worn to and from school, was perched precariously on the left-hand branches of the horns, and he didn't want to shake it off.

A little crowd of school children, some of whom had come out of their way to be first to inspect the wonderful antlers, had gathered with Melanie and Paul at the bottom of Repton Road.

Melanie was trying to be very casual about it all. 'Of course,' she said, 'Paul and I knew about it all from the start. In fact, *we* suggested the idea in the first place.'

In fact, she was as eager as the rest of them to see the latest stage in the growth of Billy's antlers and strained her eyes down the road, hoping to catch sight of him.

'If you thought of the idea first why didn't *you* grow antlers?' asked Janice Sullivan, turning to Melanie.

'Now don't be stupid,' replied Melanie, quite unperturbed by the insinuation, 'A girl would look pretty silly in antlers, wouldn't she?'

'Then why didn't you?' said Janice sharply, turning to Paul.

Paul replied that he didn't fancy antlers himself and added, when the murmurs from the crowd of children made him feel that he had said something to make himself unpopular, that he thought that Billy would look very handsome in them.

At last Billy sauntered up, trying to pretend that he didn't know that the crowd had collected for his benefit.

'Phew! How big are they, Billy?' asked Marion Phipps, in a tone of unconcealed admiration.

'Oh, about eight and a half inches from my head to the topmost point, I should think,' replied Billy, who had measured them carefully at least four times since breakfast.

Jacek Volkovinsky eyed them with envy. 'I wonder if you could take a cutting?' he said.

The children followed Billy to school, the crowd behind him gradually increasing as they approached the gates. At last they all streamed up the drive and across the playground, and came to a halt in front of the headmaster's study. Billy pulled the crumpled note from his pocket and knocked quietly on the door. A pause, and then the faint 'Come in' was heard.

Feeling as nervous as he usually felt when he had to enter the headmaster's room, Billy slid round the door as silently as he could. The headmaster, who was standing by the fireplace, went pale as he caught sight of the antlers, felt behind him for the support of his desk, tottered round it, sat down heavily in his chair, and said, in a voice as strict as he could manage in the circumstances, 'What is it, Dexter?'

'Please, sir, I've brought a note,' said Billy politely. In fact, he could easily have explained for himself, if any explanation had been necessary.

The headmaster took the piece of paper, which Billy's mother had carefully folded eight times, unfolded it with equal care and read:

Dear Mr Bartholemew,

So sorry we kept Billy away yesterday as we had to take him to the specialist on account of his bumps which he says are not catching. Will you please see to it that the other children do not tease him as he is very sensitive. There are two shillings to come back on his dinner money this week which he paid on Monday.

> *And oblige,*
> *Yours faithfully,*
> D. G. DEXTER (*Mrs*)'

The headmaster put down the note and said, in a rather weak voice, 'Thank you, Dexter; I shall have a word with Miss Beddows about it.' And with that he dismissed Billy.

Miss Beddows tried to take the news calmly, but she was clearly at a loss. For one thing, Angela Byrne and David Mailers couldn't see the board if Billy sat in his old place. And Angela kept picking the velvet off the antlers. So, much to Jacek's disappointment, Billy had to be moved to the back left-hand corner next to Tommy Mullins. He, too, picked the velvet off, but not absentmindedly like Angela. He did it so that every child in the form should have a bit as a souvenir.

Apart from these little changes, however, things went on much as before. Not quite as before, perhaps, because Billy now obviously enjoyed being in school. Gradually Miss Beddows became accustomed to the antlers, just as Mrs Dexter had done, and soon treated Billy as a normal boy again. He was able to do everything that the other children did, and there was always someone ready to lend a helping hand, when necessary, to extricate him from the climbing frame.

His antlers continued to grow. Towards the end of the term he had a magnificent head of horn, as his barber put it.

*   *   *   *

One hot afternoon the boys went out on the field to play cricket while the girls played netball on the asphalt playground. Billy was on the batting side and, as usual, he was acting as umpire so that the boys could hand him their pullovers to hang from his antlers.

'How big are they now?' asked Jacek, who was fielding at square leg.

'Just two feet, four inches from my head to the farthest tip,' replied Billy, 'and two feet, one and a half inches across at the widest point.' He always felt a glow inside when he was asked about his antlers.

'Will they just grow and grow forever?' asked the fascinated Jacek.

'Oh, I expect so,' said Billy, not caring to admit that he didn't control their progress. 'Until I want them to stop, that is,' he added.

'You mustn't stop,' said Jacek quickly. 'You must keep them growing until they weigh tonnes and tonnes.'

Now this set Billy thinking. The antlers were already quite heavy; not uncomfortably so, but he had to hold his head upright to avoid getting a crick in the neck. What if they should keep on flourishing? At the moment they were magnificent and well worth the slight inconvenience that they caused, but if they grew and grew and finally weighed tonnes and tonnes, as Jacek put it, they were going to be an embarrassment. But Billy decided that he would face that difficulty when it arose.

That evening Class 2 had to stay behind in the school hall to rehearse their items for the end-of-term concert. Mr Bartholemew had come along to watch and sat with Miss Beddows in front of the stage. She, in her extremely tactful and kind-hearted way, had arranged some English folk dances for her class, selecting Billy as a member of a team of boys who were to do a dance with antlers. The antlers should really have been held at chest level, but Miss Beddows insisted that the other boys should hold theirs on their heads, and that Billy should put his hands on his head, too. Miss Beddows liked folk dancing and her class did it every year in the school concert.

Old Mr Botterell, the school caretaker, stood ruefully surveying the props and the costumes that came out of storage at this time each year.

'That there 'obby 'orse 'as practically 'ad it, miss, if you ask me. That won't last another concert after this.'

'Never mind,' replied Miss Beddows cheerfully, 'who knows, by next year one of the boys may have grown a tail.' She really had got used to Billy's antlers, as you see.

The dancers got into line, the hobby horse, fife player and drum player stood ready at the side and Miss Beddows struck a commanding chord on the piano. Soon they were all bobbing and prancing about the stage in their own spirited version of the dance. Since there wasn't much room on the stage, it was inevitable that the antlers should get interlocked from time to time and, since Billy's were a fixture, the other boys released their hold when this happened. The music finished. The boys who had lost their antlers in the fray went up to Billy to disentangle them from his. Then they all left the stage to make way for the next group.

✳　✳　✳　✳

Billy was thirsty after a hot afternoon at cricket and then all this jumping about.

'Please, miss, may I go for a drink of water?'

'Be quick,' came the reply.

Billy scampered out of the hall and along the open verandah. There was a drinking fountain on the wall at the far end, outside the boys' cloak rooms. He bent over it from one side and let the water play over his mouth and chin for a while before drinking. Having quenched his thirst he

stood upright again and found himself looking straight across the quadrangle into the window of the headmaster's study. He could make out a figure at the far side of the room. It wasn't the headmaster because he was in the hall, but whoever it was, was touching the door of the headmaster's safe.

Billy thought that something was wrong and out of curiosity he crossed the quadrangle, which the children were forbidden to do, and took a closer look through the window. The man now had the safe open and was hurriedly stuffing whatever he could lay his hands on into a briefcase lying on the table beside him.

'It's a burglary,' thought Billy. And as quickly as he could he ran round the building to the door of the headmaster's room and hid behind the locker where the drinking straws were kept. Almost immediately the door opened and the man put his head out, looked quickly down the verandah and hurried along it on his way to the drive.

Billy didn't know what to do at first but, on the spur of the moment, he made up his mind. He rushed silently from his hiding place and sped after the retreating figure, his head held low in front of him. The man heard nothing because Billy had on his gym shoes for the folk dancing and moved very lightly. Faster and faster he went, and nearer and nearer he drew until – CRASH!

The unsuspecting man was knocked clean off his balance and fell sprawling. The bag flew from his hand and burst open several yards ahead, its contents scattering all over the ground. Billy remembered little else of that moment. He had been dazed by the blow.

When he started coming to, he found himself in the medical room and he could hear the voices of Miss Beddows and Mr Bartholemew talking about the burglary.

'The children are terribly excited about it,' Miss Beddows was saying, sounding very excited herself.

'Well, after all, this sort of thing doesn't happen every day,' replied the headmaster. 'And Dexter put up an excellent show there. That boy certainly knows how to use his head. He deserves a decoration.'

Billy wondered what sort of decoration it would be. He pictured himself with his antlers decked with tinsel and winking fairy lights, like a Christmas tree.

'He's coming round,' said Miss Beddows.

'Hello, Dexter,' said Mr Bartholemew in a loud, but friendly, voice. 'Well done. You've caught a burglar for us and we're all very grateful. Very grateful. How are you feeling?'

'I've got a bit of a headache,' said Billy.

The rehearsal was over, and when Miss Beddows asked who would see Billy safely home, sixteen children, including Melanie and Paul, eagerly volunteered. Some of them even lived in the opposite direction. And so Billy had a hero's escort back to his house that evening.

Since he still felt a little dazed and still had a headache, the doctor and the vet were summoned. They examined him carefully and assured Mrs Dexter that he had suffered no harm, but advised her to keep him at home and make him rest for the next few days.

This was sad for Billy as it meant missing the concert. It was quite a relief for Miss Beddows. She liked Billy but as she said: 'The bigger the things grew the greater the chaos on the stage during the Abbots Bromley horn dance.'

* * * *

Billy was allowed to go to see the concert with his parents. And just imagine his surprise when, at the end of the performance, the headmaster came on to the stage to tell the crowded hall about Billy's heroic deed. The parents and children all cheered and Billy had to go up on to the stage to take a bow.

His parents watched with pride from their places in the hall as Billy accepted a pen and pencil set as a gift from the headmaster and the staff for his prompt action, and their eyes filled with tears of joy as the children on the stage threw paper streamers over Billy's antlers and sang 'For He's a Jolly Good Fellow'.

After the concert Billy and a large crowd of children ran from the hall to talk things over in the summer dusk on the school playing field. No one had seen him since the evening of the burglary and so many of them wanted to hear the story from his own lips.

He scratched his head. 'It was nothing, really,' he began, scratching his head again. 'I went out for a drink of water and saw this man ...'

What was wrong with his head? It itched terribly and scratching with his fingers didn't seem to do any good. Finally he could stand it no longer.

'Excuse me,' he said, and pushed his way through the admiring crowd to the horse chestnut tree that stood at the edge of the cricket pitch. Then he pushed his head against the tree and rubbed, slowly at first, then more and more vigorously.

'Oh, Billy, be careful,' called Melanie anxiously.

Harder and harder he scratched himself against the trunk. The crowd of children stood in silence, gaping with astonishment.

'Billy!' Melanie called again.

But it was done. The itching had stopped. The antlers lay on the ground at Billy's feet. At first he couldn't believe his eyes: the antlers had simply fallen off.

Yes, Billy had lost his antlers and his disappointment was immense. The children crowded round sympathetically and gradually it became clear to Billy that although they, too, felt

the loss, it didn't really matter to them that the antlers were no longer growing.

'At least you can keep them to show people,' said Paul, consolingly.

'They'll be much easier to manage now,' said Melanie. It was true; they had been getting rather heavy. And everyone agreed that they had to come off some time and that Billy had, after all, proved his point by growing them in the first place. And everyone said that they would always remember them and the way Billy had captured the burglar with them.

The children exchanged quiet 'Good nights' and Paul, Melanie and the sad Billy went off to find their parents.

*   *   *   *

When the children returned to school after the summer holidays Billy was his normal self again and seemed, if anything, more cheerful and harder working than in the days before he grew the antlers.

This afternoon he sat engrossed in the raffia mat that he was making. He pulled a piece of purple raffia from the tangle of coloured raffia in front of him and began to thread it carefully, over and under, over and under.

Miss Sloane, their new teacher, walked slowly up and down, between the rows of desks, picking up a raffia mat here and there. Suddenly the silence was broken by an exclamation of disgust from Miss Sloane. Jacek Volkovinsky shrank wretchedly in his seat.

'Just look at *that*, Jacek Volkovinsky,' Miss Sloane burst out. 'I've never seen such an untidy, messy …' As she spoke she tore out the strands of raffia, dropping them one by one on the desk in front of Jacek.

'It's not as if you can't do better. You can do very neat work if you try. If you'd only concentrate you could make a perfectly good raffia mat.'

Miss Sloane walked out to the front again. 'You just don't try. That's the trouble with *you*, Jacek Volkovinsky; you don't try,' she concluded.

Melanie Pearce put the finishing touches to her mat, placed it on the desk in front of her, winked at Billy who was sitting next to her and tapped Jacek on the shoulder. 'Bet you couldn't grow a trunk,' she said.

First published in 1961 by Faber and Faber Limited
and in 2002 by Barn Owl Books

This edition published in 2018
by Thames & Hudson Ltd

The Boy Who Sprouted Antlers © 2018 Thames & Hudson Ltd
Foreword © 2018 Quentin Blake
Text © 1961, 2002 and 2018 John Yeoman
Illustrations © 1961, 2002 and 2018 Quentin Blake

All Rights Reserved. No part of this publication may be
reproduced or transmitted in any form or by any means,
electronic or mechanical, including photocopy, recording
or any other information storage and retrieval system,
without prior permission in writing from the publisher.

British Library Cataloguing-in-Publication Data
A catalogue record for this book is available from
the British Library

ISBN 978-0-500-65160-5

Printed and bound in China by C & C Offset Printing Co. Ltd

To find out about all our publications, please visit
www.thamesandhudson.com. There you can
subscribe to our e-newsletter, browse or download
our current catalogue, and buy any titles that are in print.